AF406809

CONTENTS

Lockdown Master

Hugh Everett

1 A VERY PERSONAL TRAINER

It had been an eventful year for Adam. He had sold his online marketing business to a competitor, expecting to have to stay on for 2 years. After 3 months, the new owners felt that it would be better for him to leave sooner rather than later to give the new Managing Director free reign. He was therefore sitting on a pile of cash and had signed a contract agreeing not to work in the industry for at least a year.

The unexpected free time gave Adam lots of time to think about life in general and his plan to buy an It had been an eventful year for Adam. He had sold his apartment and move in with Luke, his partner of 2 years, didn't seem like such a good idea upon closer inspection. It wasn't so much that they had drifted apart as drifted into friendship. The passion had definitely waned and Adam feared that moving in together would kill off their sex life altogether.

Adam picked their regular Friday night date at a local brasserie to break the news that he did not want them to move in together. After a couple of cocktails for Dutch courage, Adam launched into his prepared speech about their future together. He expected a shocked reaction, maybe even tears, but instead a look of pure relief spread over Luke's face as he realised where Adam was heading and he blurted out "I've been thinking the same thing, I just didn't know how to tell you." Now it was Luke's turn to look relieved. He was truly glad not to be leaving Luke heartbroken.

"Let's face it, Adam," Luke continued, "we're both looking for the same thing in the bedroom – the other guy to take charge – and neither of us are that masterful." Adam, as the notional top in their relationship, was about to protest that he could be masterful in the sack, but before he could speak, Luke held up his hand. "Don't start pretending you're all dom now, Adam – I've seen your browsing history and there are quite a lot of pornos with a certain leather Master telling his slave boy EXACTLY what he's going to do him." Adam blushed, then laughed and called for more drinks.

Two months later Adam collected the keys to his new riverside apartment, free as a bird and ready to use his remaining gardening leave to launch himself back into the gay scene. The problem was, moving in day was 7th March 2020 and unbeknownst to him, his freedom would only last 2 weeks before the Covid lockdown spoilt all his plans.

By the third week of lockdown, Adam had had enough. He was bored of Zoom quizzes, was drinking too much and putting on weight with the excess of baked goods that everyone seemed to be producing. He was also horny as hell and seemed to have gone through the whole Pornhub catalogue. His only salvation was his daily bike ride – allowed as his permitted form of exercise.

After one afternoon ride to the south side of the Thames,

Adam was securing his bike in the underground car park of his apartment block, when a tall figure emerged from the shadows. Adam stopped in his tracks, one end of his bike lock still in his hand. He stared at the profusely sweating muscle god who was ambling towards him. "I see we've both taken advantage of our exercise window today" said the smiling stranger, whilst mopping his brow with a small towel that hung from his wide shoulders. Adam was too busy staring at the man's chest and the rivulets of sweat running down to his already soaked vest to reply, so the stranger continued, "I'm really missing weight training while the gyms are closed so I've been doing resistance bands down here instead."

Adam finally pulled himself together enough to speak, "well it looks like it's working," he ventured. The man laughed, "you have to work harder at my age to keep the form." Adam dragged his eyes upwards to study the man's face. It was hard to tell his age, but a few lines round his twinkly hazel eyes suggested mid to late forties – 10 years older than Adam.

Adam was in a bit of a daze for the rest of the conversation, but he recalled a few key pieces of information as he headed up to his apartment. The Adonis-like neighbour was called Dan and he had offered to give Adam some training tips on losing the lockdown weight and building some muscle. His right arm muscles got a mini workout as soon as he got home when he threw off his shorts and wanked about Dan towering over him, ordering "Gimme 20 more."

The next morning, Adam was enjoying a leisurely coffee

on his balcony when he spotted Dan walking his dog in the communal gardens. Every so often he would do a stretch after throwing the dog her ball and managed to look gracefully athletic while totally masculine. Just looking at him made Adam's cock stir, but his horny daydream was rudely interrupted by a pretty, petite blond woman coming out of the apartment building and blowing a kiss over to Dan. Damn it, a girlfriend! Adam had assumed his sexy neighbour was straight, but had indulged himself in an elaborate fantasy, where Dan was locked down alone, horny and would maybe agree to Adam sucking him off until he was free to visit girls again. He could just imagine Dan saying in his slightly cockney accent, "I'm not gay, mate, but you get bored with wanking, dontcha? And you are pretty good at it."

Adam moped around for 2 days and then got so bored he decided to start a fitness regime. After a smoothie he headed out into the communal garden for some press ups in the sun. After only about 15 he was already struggling and realised how unfit he had become. He determined to get to at least 50, but was only half way through when a shadow engulfed him and he saw 2 trainers on the ground directly in front of him. He looked up to see a grinning Dan, muscles rippling under a white vest. "Looks like you need a bit more practice" Dan observed, stepping forward so that his feet were directly under Adam's head. "We used to do this in the army if someone was flagging" continued Dan. "If you didn't keep your arms strong, you ended up kissing your mate's sweaty boots, or in this case trainers."

Adam blushed. As if Dan couldn't get any sexier, turned out he was an ex-soldier! Unlike Dan's old army buddies, Adam couldn't think of anything he would rather do at that moment than kiss the size 11 Pumas in front of him. He was still poised awkwardly at Dan's feet when he felt a strong arm under his, helping him to stand. "Come up to mine and we'll start on those tips I mentioned" he said when Adam was almost at eye level. "Won't your girlfriend mind you bringing a sweaty bloke back unannounced?" Adam replied. Dan looked puzzled, then grinned again. "Ah you saw Kelly the other day. She doesn't live with me – she just popped round for some clothes she had left. She lives with her sister who has asthma, so we have to be really careful."

Best news I've heard all day, thought Adam as he followed Dan back into the building.

2 DAN, THE ALPHA MALE

As they entered the apartment, Adam tore his eyes away from Dan's tanned, muscled shoulders to take in the open plan kitchen / living area. Typical straight bachelor pad, he thought to himself – white walls, tan leather sofa, huge TV and some terrible art that looked like it had been bought as a holiday souvenir.

He felt a strong hand on his back as Dan gently propelled him to a corner of the room set up as a workout space with weights and a yoga mat. "Might as well carry on with the press ups" announced Dan, nodding at the yoga mat. It wasn't quite the "get down and gimme 20" that Adam had imagined in his wank fantasy, but Dan's proximity and his deep, confident voice made his dick twitch in his shorts. He got down on the mat and started the press ups. After 5, he felt a gentle pressure on his back and looked up to see that Dan was resting his foot on him. Dan chuckled and said, "we don't want to make it too easy for you, do we?"

After another 30, Adam was a flagging again and he felt Dan's foot lift off his back and heard 2 gentle thuds as his neighbour's trainers were kicked off onto the wood floor. He came round and stood under Adam's head. "I thought we'd give you more of an incentive. If you don't keep up the press ups properly you will find your face in my sweaty gym socks." Adam was grateful that he was still face down on the mat, as the sight and smell of Dan's clean, but damp white socks made him instantly hard. After 20 more reps, his arms were genuinely shaking as his face did brush against the cotton and it took all his will power not to kiss Dan's foot that was so temptingly close to his lips. Dan chuckled again and told Adam that was enough for today.

Adam looked up at the 6'2" hunk towering over him with a mixture of relief for his aching arms and disappointment that his face was no longer going to be within inches of Dan's feet. As if reading his mind, Dan said, "Although, if you like my feet that much, they could do with a rub – I had a run before I met you in the garden." Adam searched Dan's expression. Had he been too obvious in ogling this straight guy's feet? Was this some kind of test? Trying not to sound too eager, he said, "well you've helped with my training, I owe you one." Dan grinned as he sauntered over to the large, L-shaped sofa and made himself comfortable, spreading his tanned, muscular legs out in front of him. Adam followed and knelt on the soft rug by Dan's right foot, gently lifted into his lap and started working his sole with his thumbs through the damp cotton. He was immediately rewarded with appreciative groans from Dan.

He glanced up at Dan's face and saw that he had his eyes closed, enjoying the treatment. After about 10 minutes, he couldn't resist suggesting to Dan that he take his sock off to give the most effective massage. Dan lazily opened his eyes and nodded. Adam gently peeled off the sock to reveal a beautiful, tanned, hairless foot with a couple of raised veins across the bridge and long toes with neatly clipped nails. He worked the sole with the knuckles of one hand whilst applying slight pressure to the bridge, eliciting more groans of pleasure from Dan. He finished the right foot by gently pulling each toe in turn, having to desperately fight the urge to suck them and lick the sweat from in between. "Left one now?" he asked Dan quietly. Dan opened his eyes again and made to pull his foot from Adam's hand, but suddenly changed direction and lowered it to press against Adam's very hard cock. Adam glanced down in disbelief and only at that moment realised he had been leaking so much precum that a wet patch had formed on the front of his shorts. Beet red, he looked up and felt Dan's eyes bore into him. He was convinced he was going to be kicked out and denounced as a filthy fag, but Dan just smiled enigmatically, lifted his bare right foot from Adam's lap and replaced it with the still socked left one. Adam's heart was pounding and his cock no less hard, so in the absence of any order to the contrary, he started the same massage routine on the proffered left foot.

He finished in the same way, pulling each toe and then gently resting Dan's foot in his lap. He looked up questioningly at Dan, having no idea where this whole scene was heading. "Thank you, you did a great job," said Dan slowly. "I liked doing it," replied Adam very quietly, head down. "I can tell," said Dan, grinning and rubbing his foot once again on Adam's hard on. He lifted his foot away and patted the sofa beside him as a signal for Adam to get up and sit next to him.

"I suppose you want to know what is going to happen

next?" he asked, glancing around at Adam, then turning to look straight ahead. "Yes please," said Adam meekly.

Still looking ahead, not at Adam, Dan continued, "Well….as you guys would say, I *identify* as straight." The word 'identify' was said in an ironic tone as if it were far too much pyscho-babble for a macho, straight bloke like him. "But, this thing happened in the army. My best mate and me did this taster course for transferring to the SAS. One part of the course was PoW treatment and interrogation techniques. Your team mates draw lots – 2 guys get to be the captors and 2 the prisoners. Luckily my mate Stu and me both drew the captor cards and we had 3 hours to get info out of the 'prisoners.' Only rules were you had to stick to the Geneva Convention – no torture, no sexual abuse, no food, water or sleep deprivation. So Stu goes for the humiliation technique – had the prisoners kissing his boots, even pissed on one of them. I played the good cop and we won the exercise by getting all the prisoners to spill all the beans. Stu got taken aside after and told that 'whilst effective, his techniques were not in tune with the SAS ethos.' Thing was, the power over another guy really turned me on. I was so fucking horny after the course, the bird I was seeing got the fuck of her life as soon as I got back home. I still think of it sometimes and Kelly likes a bit of mild domination – those fluffy pink hand cuffs you see in sex shops – stuff like that." Dan paused, still staring straight ahead. Adam remained silent, looking at the chiselled profile of the ex-soldier beside him and waited for him to continue.

Eventually he did. "Then I met you in the car park. You were trying not to show it, but the lust was written all over your face and…" Another long pause. "I got this feeling you would love me to have total control over you." He finally looked back round at Adam. "Am I right?" Adam couldn't form any words, but nodded his assent.

"So, what is going to happen now is you are going to go back to yours, where I am sure you are dying to wank over our little scene here. However, you are not allowed to wank until you go to bed tonight and then tomorrow morning you are going to write me a long and detailed email of exactly what you were fantasizing about." He grabbed Adam's arm with one hand, reached for a pen with the other and wrote his email address on his wrist.

"Now, fuck off home" was Dan's not so polite goodbye.

3 ADAM'S LETTER

Adam left Dan's flat and put his hands in front of his shorts to hide the wet spot. Luckily there were no other neighbours in the corridors or lift. He closed his own front door and breathed a sigh of relief. He shucked off his wet shorts and his still raging boner slapped against his stomach, leaving a few drops of pre cum. He was confused and shocked after the scene in Dan's flat, but hornier than he had ever been in his life. His cock ached to be touched, but he daren't even brush his hand against it in case it triggered an orgasm. It was only 10.30 am and he wondered if his will power would last until bedtime. It didn't even occur to him to disobey Dan's instructions. After only two brief meetings, all he wanted to do was please the ex-army stud.

He took a cold shower and re-dressed in boxers, jeans and a sweater, figuring that the more layers between his hand and his cock, the less his temptation there would be to wank. He went through every stage of this morning's encounter, trying to remember each word Dan had uttered. It made his cock hard again, recalling the foot massage he had given. His phrase about Adam loving Dan to have total control over him replayed over and over in his mind. It was mad. Adam barely knew this guy, but the more he thought about it, the more he realised it was true.

The began to wonder what 'total control' entailed. Dan had already decided when Adam was allowed to wank. Would he have to get Dan's permission any time he wanted to touch himself? Would he have to ask to leave his own flat?

Then there was the conundrum about Dan 'identifying as straight' but being massively turned on by having another guy under his control. Did that mean that he wouldn't get to suck Dan or be fucked by him – just hang around to take orders? The thought that he might not even get to see Dan's cock made him shudder.

Adam looked at his watch. He had been pacing around his flat for 2 hours, thinking of nothing but Dan. He pulled himself together a bit, had a sandwich and then went out for a bike ride to clear his head. By three pm he was back in the flat, horny again and thinking non-stop about Dan. He watched some movies and got to 9.30pm before he could hold off no longer. He slowly undressed and lay naked on his bed. Would Dan consider it too early to count as bedtime? He wasn't 11 years old after all. Well, too late. He was hard and naked and he just couldn't help himself any longer. He scooped some of the precum off his glistening knob and sucked it off his fingers, wondering what Dan's would taste like. He thought of Dan's muscled legs spread wide on his sofa and the feel and smell of his beautiful feet. Within seconds he was shooting a rope of cum over his shoulder onto the pillow, swiftly followed another that landed on his hairy forearm.

He fell into a contented sleep, but was wide awake at 2am, hard again. He began to gently stroke his cock, thinking about Dan's next instruction – the email he was to write in the morning. Soon he was shooting his load again, not so violently as before, but still powerfully.

Since the lockdown began, Adam had been sleeping in late, enjoying the freedom of not having to work, but the next morning, he was at the desk, laptop open, by 8am. Yesterday's cold shower had faded the email address on his wrist, but it was still legible. Just looking at Dan's writing on his skin made Adam's cock twitch. He began to type:

"Dear Dan,

I did what you said and waited until yesterday evening before wanking about our meeting. It was so hard to wait that long as I was crazily horny after seeing you.

Holding off cumming did give me a LOT of time to fantasise though. Maybe that was your intention?"

Adam stopped typing and stared at the screen. Some of the scenarios he had thought about the day before might freak straight-identifying Dan out. They were definitely gay fantasies. After a long pause, he began to type again

"You were very honest with me yesterday about the interrogation thing and about Kelly, so I'm going to be honest with you, even though I am scared you will think I am a massive perv and never want to see me again.

You were right – I was lusting after you in the car park. You are so handsome and masculine and your body is so hot. I fancy everything about you from that curly hair and twinkly hazel eyes down to your perfect feet. You are also right that I wanted you to be in charge straight away; to tell me what to do and how to please you.

Yesterday, while I was massaging your feet, I was desperate to kiss and lick them. I wanted to suck your toes. I wanted to kiss up your legs until I got to your balls. I wanted you to nod at me to tell me it was OK to worship your balls with my tongue and then have me beg to taste your cock and swallow it down my throat"

Adam paused again. His heart was pounding. Would the thought of a grown man begging Dan to suck his dick turn him on or repulse him? He thought about deleting the last paragraph, but decided to plunge on.

"Of course, from the little you said yesterday, I have no idea if you would like what I just wrote, but you ordered me to tell you about my fantasies and that was definitely up there. I have thought about it a lot and I really, really want to please you, even if that means just kneeling at your feet waiting for orders or running around serving you, not necessarily in a sexual way.

I want it to be about you, Sir, and your pleasure (another fantasy is to call you Sir).

I hope I have not put you off and would love to see you again whenever you are ready, Sir.

Respectfully Yours

Adam"

Adam pressed send. 'Please let him like it, he whispered to himself as he closed the laptop.

4 A FANTASY COMES TRUE

Dan was awake early as usual and took himself for a run and then back into the communal garden of the apartment block for some cool down stretches. Back in his flat he had a leisurely shower, made a healthy breakfast and then checked his emails. There were a couple of work messages to attend to, but as most of his personal security work had dried up during lockdown, it did not take long. He switched to the personal email he had given Adam and was pleased to see a message timed at 08.30 from his obedient neighbour.

He had been thinking about Adam a lot since their encounter yesterday. He had surprised himself by opening up so candidly to a man he hardly knew. The only gay experiences he had had were a few drunken army initiation ceremonies where forfeits had included kissing another guy's arse or having to peel back their foreskin.

The episode about getting turned on by his friend humiliating other soldiers in a training session had led to a few wanks, but he hadn't thought about it leading to actual sex with another man. There was something about Adam though, that made Dan question himself. Adam was a good looking guy, and the way he looked so blissed out while kneeling, massaging his feet as well as the physical sensation of his hands, gave Dan immense pleasure. After Adam had left, Dan realised he was half hard and pulled down his shorts while still on the sofa. He slowly stroked his thick, uncut cock until the pre-cum was oozing out of his piss slit. He looked down at his own feet and imagined Adam still on his knees, looking up expectantly and surprised himself by suddenly shooting an impressive load over his defined chest. As he squeezed the last few drops of spunk out of his cock head, he shuddered. What was this Adam guy doing to him? He hadn't planned to ejaculate there on the sofa, so had to waddle to the bathroom with his shorts still round his ankles trying not to let the cooling jizz drip onto the rug.

Thinking about this the next day, Adam's unopened e-mail sitting in front of him on the screen, Dan hesitated. He was excited and curious to see exactly what Adam had written, but wary about getting too involved with a gay guy. Maybe he should just delete Adam's message without even reading it and suggest a bit of cam sex with the isolating Kerry instead. While he was still pondering, his phone rang – a client from Monaco checking the quarantine regulations for the security guys Dan's company were providing. By the time he'd finished the call and done some further checking for the client it was lunchtime. He didn't get back to his laptop until 2pm and, having nothing else to do, he decided to go for it and read Adam's email.

He read it twice and, by the time he got to Adam's sentence "I want it to be about you, Sir, and your pleasure' for the second time, he was as hard as a rock, his erection tenting the jogging bottoms that were his usual lockdown attire.

In the army, only the officers were addressed as 'Sir.' He was just 'Sarge.' The fact that Adam fantasised about calling him Sir was a massive turn on. He started stroking himself through the cotton of his joggers as he imagined Adam's educated voice saying 'please may I suck your cock, Sir?'

One floor up and 5 apartments along, Adam had been like a cat on a hot tin roof for over 6 hours since he sent the email to Dan. He hadn't expected an instant response, but the continued silence was killing him. He couldn't put his phone down and had been checking his inbox constantly since midday. He wondered over and over how Dan would have reacted. Would he be appalled, shocked, turned on?

He was pacing around his kitchen, barely able to concentrate on making a cup of tea when the doorbell rang. Thinking it was the concierge with a parcel, he opened the door with a smile, to be faced with the imposing figure of former Sergeant Daniel Russell. He looked into Dan's unsmiling eyes, but couldn't read his expression. He lowered his gaze, not daring to speak. Dan took a step forward into the hall and Adam stepped aside to let him.

"Close the door," Dan ordered. Adam did as he was told, stomach knotting at the authoritative tone. As soon as the door was shut behind him, Dan issued his second command: "on your knees." Adam felt frozen to the spot. He was expecting Dan to talk about the email or to remind him that he was straight. Seeing no action, Dan spoke very slowly, "I said….get….on…..your….fucking…..knees."

This time Adam obeyed immediately, taking in Dan's tented joggers, bare ankles and black leather trainers on the way down. He glanced up at Dan's chiselled face, but the intensity of his stare seemed too much and he immediately lowered his eyes back to the trainers. Dan remained silent for a long moment, then continued, "you wanted to ask me something.." Adam looked up again, confused. His brain had turned to mush. "Or should I say, you wanted to *beg* for something," prompted the deep voice from above. Adam suddenly realised Dan was referring to his email – he knew it almost by heart as he has re-read it so many times before and after sending it. He blushed and stuttered before beginning the speech he had fantasised about. "Please Sir, may I taste your cock. I really need it Sir. I want to please you. I'm begging for the honour of sucking it, Sir."

With each 'Sir,' Adam saw Dan's bulge grow a bit more. He looked up again and saw Dan give the slightest of nods. Still on his knees, he lent forward and kissed Dan's hard cock through the thick cotton of the joggers. He kissed up and down the covered shaft several times before tentatively reaching for Dan's waistband. He looked up enquiringly and received another nod. As he pulled the fabric down, Dan's impressive 8" cock bounced out. It was smooth and pale, with 2 veins running up the shaft and a generous foreskin that was already peeled pack from a leaking head. His pubes were neatly trimmed and his large balls shaved smooth. Adam repeated the same kissing pattern up and down the now naked shaft, taking in the addictive mix of clean, slightly soapy skin and precum.

He reached out his tongue to see if the precum tasted as good as it smelled, but Dan's large, freckled hand grabbed his thick, dark hair. Dan tilted Adam's head back until their eyes met. "I think you mentioned my balls in your email. Get to it," he ordered.

Adam didn't need telling twice and started lapping at Dan's balls, savouring the taste and smell with each lick. Dan's hand was still on his head, but with less pressure so that Adam was able to reach every part of the low hanging flesh with his eager tongue. It didn't take long for Dan to start moaning with pleasure and he moved his hand from Adam's head to his own cock and began slowly stroking himself, spreading his copious precum up and down his shaft. Adam pulled away and looked up expectantly. Dan looked down, nodded once again and removed his hand to give his neighbour's hungry mouth access to his knob.

Adam, desperate to make the most of this precious time with a straight ex-soldier, tried out his technique of tonguing round Dan's cock head, then suddenly swallowing as much of the shaft as he could in one go. The quiet "fuuuuuuck" from Dan, let him know that his efforts were appreciated. On the third round of tonguing and swallowing, Adam felt Dan's strong hand on top of his head once more, pushing him further down the rock hard shaft. He wasn't prepared for this and began to gag. Dan's vice like grip held him in place for a few more seconds, then allowed him some leeway to take a breath. Keen not to disappoint the stud towering over him, Adam began to tongue his cockhead once more whilst wanking his shaft.

Dan came so suddenly and violently that some of his spunk went up Adam's nose, causing him to cough and trail Dan's seed down his chin and T-shirt. He looked up to see a puzzled expression on Dan's face as if he had startled himself with the speed and strength of his own orgasm. He took his hand from Adam's head and used it to tuck his cock back into his joggers. "Stay there on your knees until my spunk dries on you" were Dan's parting words as he reached for the front door handle.

5 DON'T MAKE ME GAY

Adam did as he was told, savouring the smell of Dan's spunk as it slowly dripped down his chin and neck. He remained on his knees and, despite his raging boner, did not touch his cock until the semen was dry enough to peel off in flakes. He still felt in a kind of trance when he shifted from his kneeling position to lay on his back on the hall floor, but could no longer resist the urge to stroke his aching dick and within a minute shot so hard that some of his hot, fresh seed landed on his face, mingling with the residue of Dan's. After resting on the floor for quite a while longer, he dragged himself up and started to run a bath.

One floor down, Dan was sitting at his kitchen island, staring out at the river. His mind was racing. He had just experienced one of the most powerful orgasms of his life, but it was with a man. It wasn't right. He was straight. He liked to fuck pussy and play with tits. He thought of Kelly. She didn't mind giving him blow jobs now and again, but she didn't seem to relish it like Adam. And those things he did with his tongue….

He hadn't been drinking during lockdown, but he needed something to calm him down now. He poured a healthy measure of whisky and sat back down at the island. 2 hours and half a bottle later, far from being calm, he was raging. That gay boy Adam had seduced him. Caught him

at a time when he couldn't see his girlfriend. He was a
fucking opportunist. Dan's drunken logic left out the key
elements that it was he who had invited Adam back to his,
had suggested the foot massage and had ordered a hesitant
Adam onto his knees. He slammed his empty tumbler
down on the counter and headed upstairs to Adam's flat.

After his bath, Adam was relaxed, but couldn't concentrate
on anything other than Dan, so was just sitting in his
dressing gown, listening to Motown and trying to convince
himself not to fall in love with his unavailable, straight
neighbour. The ring at his door made him jump and he
cautiously opened the front door to see a red faced and
slightly swaying Dan standing in the corridor. Dan lunged
in, slamming the door behind him. "I need a word with
you. We need to sort this out" he said menacingly, shoving
Adam in the chest with each sentence. "But I thought you
liked it?" replied Adam, his voice faltering. "Of course I
fucking liked it. What bloke doesn't like a blow job. But
I'm not fucking gay!" Dan was shouting by now, still
shoving Adam further into the flat with every few words.
Adam could now smell the whisky on Dan's breath and
was scared that he was really out of control. He turned
away, thinking he could maybe dart into his bedroom and
lock himself in. Dan grabbed the collar of Adam's
dressing gown and it came off completely as Adam rushed
forward into the bedroom.

Dan followed him over the threshold before he could
close the door and the now naked Adam stood cowering
in front of his taller, stronger, ex-army neighbour. Dan
stepped closer until Adam was backed up against the
bottom of the bed. He started shouting again, "You're

trying to make me fucking gay." Despite his fear, Adam couldn't help laughing at this ridiculous statement. In this case laughter did not diffuse the situation. Dan started screaming "DON'T LAUGH AT ME." With one hard shove, Adam was knocked back onto the bed. Dan then spotted a belt that Adam had taken off earlier, grabbed it and started lashing at Adam's naked body. Adam tried to crawl towards the top of the bed to escape from the rain of blows, but it only exposed his buttocks as an easy target for Dan. Dan ignored his demands to stop and it was only when Adam begged, "please, SIR, it hurts too much" that Dan stopped in his tracks. It was as if 'Sir' was the magic word that brought Dan out of his drunken fury. He slumped on the bed, letting the belt fall to the floor. "I'm drunk," he murmured, before passing out.

Adam was still in shock. Dan had turned from an exciting lover to a violent attacker in a matter of hours and was now gently snoring on his bed. Even after what just happened, Adam couldn't help staring at the fine specimen of manhood that was lying next to him. The sting of the belting had already worn off and the warm ache the welts left behind were actually a kind of sexy reminder of Dan's power. Adam took himself into the bathroom to examine his backside. It was red and he could see the marks that the belt had left. Somehow his shock and fear melted away and he almost felt proud that his body was carrying the marks Dan had given him.

Adam went back to check on Dan, who was still snoring. He didn't want to risk his anger again by trying to wake him, but couldn't bring himself to go into the other room, so lay on his stomach on the bed (his arse still felt too tender to have any weight on it) watching Dan's muscular chest rise and fall with each breath until he drifted off to sleep.

At 6am Dan woke. He opened his eyes, puzzled. The bedroom was the same layout as his, but the walls were a different colour. He moved his head to look around, but this ignited his hangover and he groaned with the pain that shot behind his eyes. After a few more minutes shuteye, he attempted another look around the room, more slowly this time. His gaze soon fell upon the naked body of Adam next to him, complete with now quite bruised buttocks. "Holy fuck, what have I done?" he said to himself, but loud enough to wake Adam.

Adam raised his head sleepily to look at Dan. He looked scared, unsure what mood his neighbour had woken in. Dan sat up, the memories of last night's outburst rushing back into his consciousness. "I am so sorry," he said contritely, forcing himself to look Adam in the eye. "I hadn't had a drink for weeks and I…I wqs so confused and then I hit the whisky….and then I hit you." He looked as if he would cry, but his military training kicked in and he pulled himself together.

"It's OK," said Adam, reaching out his hand tentatively to rest it on Dan's forearm. Dan didn't pull away, so he decided to continue. "I don't know how to say this without making you mad again, but I think there is kind of a range – you know, from straight to gay and.." he paused, carefully considering his words "..and it's not like the old days where you had to be labelled. It's possible that you get – one gets – turned on by certain things with a woman and other things with a man. It doesn't mean you have to change your whole identity."

Dan was listening very carefully, nodding slowly in agreement. "I shouldn't have done that to you though," he said, reaching out to very gently touch Adam's bruised buttock." The light touch of Dan's strong hand sent a bolt of electricity through his whole body and his cock was instantly rock hard against the mattress. 'Shit,' he thought to himself, 'showing off my morning wood is not going to help with Dan's homophobia.' Out loud he said, "why don't you have a shower. Clear your head. Then we can talk if you want."

Dan thought this was a great idea. Adam lay in bed, listening to the shower run in the en-suite and imagined Dan's naked body with the water streaming over it.

10 minutes later, Dan came back out, golden chest hair still a bit damp, with a towel wrapped around his waist. He was holding a bottle in his right hand. He smiled shyly and said "I found some Aloe Vera lotion. Thought it might help with that," pointing to Adam's bruised arse. "I think it might…Sir," replied dam, grinning from ear to ear."

6 THE RULES

Much to Adam's surprise, instead of just handing him the Aloe Vera, Dan climbed onto the bed next to him and squeezed some of the lotion on to his bruised arse cheeks. The combination of the cool lotion and Dan's strong hand gently massaging it in felt like absolute bliss to Adam – well worth the pain of the previous night's belting. He was still hard from imagining Dan naked in the shower and now he felt like his erection was drilling into the mattress.

For a big, muscled guy, Dan was surprisingly tender and when Adam dared to look round over his shoulder, he saw a look of intense concentration on Dan's face. He could hardly believe that his backside, albeit quite a cute one, was the focus of this straight stud's attention. After 10 minutes of careful massage, Dan lay on his side next to Adam and asked if he was OK. "That was amazing, thank you," replied Adam, genuinely grateful. "It was the least I could do, said Dan, "I was the fucking idiot who lost the plot and hurt you in the first place."

Adam took a deep breath. It seemed to him that it was one of those now-or-never moments where what he had to say would either send Dan running for the hills or lead to the best sexual adventure ever. "Last night was scary because you were drunk and angry, but…" Adam tailed off, trying to find the right words. "But, in general, I like the idea of you belting me, or spanking me. Showing me who is boss." He hadn't dared look Dan in the eye as he was talking, but he glanced up after the word 'boss' to see what Dan's reaction was. Dan had a look of delighted disbelief like a kid at Christmas who has just unwrapped the present he dreamed of, but didn't think the parents could afford.

Dan paused for a while, then started speaking very slowly, "so for example, if I had a bad day at work, I could come round here, order you to strip and assume the position and give you a good leathering to vent my frustrations?"

Adam nodded, blushing. "So what's in it for you?" Dan asked. "Well, maybe it would turn you on to beat me and I could suck you off after – to thank you for my punishment." Dan grinned and adjusted the now tenting towel that was still around his waist. "Well, you had your beating last night, boy, and I still haven't had my thank you blow job," he said, undoing the towel to reveal his hard on. "Sorry Sir," replied Adam, before wrapping his lips around Darren's beautiful cock. Dan lay back to enjoy an expert servicing from his eager neighbour, letting Adam show off his skills without the need for too much instruction. This time Adam was prepared for Darren's load and savoured the taste of soldier spunk in his mouth before swallowing it down before licking Darren's knob completely clean.

After taking a few minutes to recover from his orgasm, Dan got all straight and business-like again, getting out of bed and scouring the floor for his discarded clothes and trainers. "See you around," he said over his shoulder as he loped out of the bedroom.

Adam lay back on the bed, analysing how much to hope for from the noncommittal 'see you around,' but then his immediate need for release overtook his concerns about the future and he had a rapid, but very satisfying wank that ended in his hairy chest being covered in his own jizz.

It was to be the first of several wanks over the next two days. Two days with no word from Dan! It took all Adam's willpower not to text or email. The silence was killing him and he wished he had some work to do to stop him obsessing over his sexy neighbour. Finally, he received a longed-for text from Dan 'can we talk?' 'Sure' replied Adam with unseemly speed. 'Be at yours at midday' was Dan's response.

Dan hadn't deliberately kept Adam hanging for 2 whole days. He was still confused. Whenever he wasn't working or working out, he was mulling over the Adam situation. On reflexion, what Adam had said made sense – that you don't have to change your whole identity to enjoy what turns you on, whether that is with a woman or a man. Dan still had his doubts though. Adam seemed pretty keen on him and he was a neighbour – what if he made a scene in the lobby? What if he told Kerry when she was allowed to visit again?

From his army training and then recruiting for his private security company, Dan thought he was a pretty good judge of character and, from what little he had seen of him, Adam seemed a decent bloke. He would have to set strict parameters, of course, but he reckoned that the stricter he was, the more Adam would like it. Nothing wrong with sugaring the pill though, he thought as he dug some old army gear out of the back of his wardrobe.

Adam's doorbell rang at exactly midday and he opened the door to see Dan dressed in old army combat trousers, a khaki vest and the shiniest black boots Adam had ever seen. A large army duffle bag was slung casually over his shoulder. Adam was speechless with lust and silently ushered Dan into his flat.

Dan did not beat around the bush, "I've been thinking about this a lot and if we are going to keep seeing each other, there have to be rules." Adam nodded. Still silent, his eyes soaking in every inch of the 6'2" stud before him.

"Rule 1 – whenever I come in here, you show respect by kissing my boots or whatever I'm wearing on my feet. Get to it."

Adam was on his hands and knees in a flash, giving each boot a single kiss. The smell of the boot polish was strong and the leather so shiny that he could see a distorted reflection of his own face in the toecaps. He raised himself back on to his knees and stared adoringly up at Dan.

"Rule 2 – this remains absolutely secret. You tell NO ONE. Understood"

"Yes Sir. Of course Sir,' replied Adam in the steadiest voice his nerves would allow.

"Rule 3 – No pestering. You are not to call or text me without permission. I will see you ONLY when I want to."

Another 'Yes Sir' affirmed Adam's agreement.

"Rule 4 – no other blokes for you – you are exclusively mine until I decide otherwise"

Adam couldn't imagine any guy that would tempt him away from Dan, but kept his remarks to a 'Yes Sir.'

"Rule 5 – you follow all my orders to the letter, swiftly and respectfully. Any infractions will be punished.

A final 'Yes Sir' from Adam sealed the deal and Dan dropped the commanding, official tone he had used to recite the rules. He said softly, "Stand up. You're a good boy" and reached round into his duffle bag to produce a well worn, but clean jockstrap. "Get into the bedroom, strip and put this on. Report back to me in the living room."

Adam was back in the living room in under 2 minutes. The jock was a bit on the large side, but his erection ensured that the pouch was well filled and the faded cotton already displayed the first spot of precum. Dan had moved a dining chair into the middle of the room and was fishing some rope out of his army bag. He glanced up at Adam and nodded his head towards the chair. "Interrogation time," he announced, grinning.

7 THE INTERROGATION

Adam sat down in the chair, feeling the textured fabric of the seat pad against his bare arse and the cool wood under his forearms. Dan worked swiftly and skilfully to secure Adam's wrists to the arm rests with one length of rope and then crouched down to fasten each ankle to a front leg with a second rope. He stood back to admire his handywork and looked Adam up and down. The bulge in the borrowed jockstrap had diminished a little. Adam was still massively turned on, but the nervousness at being entirely at Dan's mercy was kicking in.

Dan stepped forward, grabbed Adam by the hair and jerked his neck back so that he was looking directly into his neighbour's eyes. "So, we can do this the easy way, or the hard way. Easy way will be quicker, but I'll probably enjoy the hard way better. I doubt you will enjoy it so much."

Adam had seen enough war movies to know the drill about name, rank and serial number, so looking Dan straight in the eye, he replied, "Adam Kingston, Private, 13071976…Sir." The 'Sir' was dripping with irony to show he had scant respect for his captor. A flicker of a smile crossed Dan's handsome face before he got back into character. "Hard way it is then," he said, fishing a riding crop out of his capacious army duffle bag.

The first stroke, on Adam's left pec, stung but was easily bearable. The second, harder and directly on his right nipple had him gripping the arms of the chair to keep his composure. "Ready to talk now?" enquired Dan in an amused tone. Adam shook his head. Dan moved the crop very slowly down Adam's hairy chest, keeping the little black square of leather at its end constantly in contact with Adam's tingling flesh. He paused when the leather reached the waistband of the jockstrap, then stroked it very gently over the pouch, which began to expand rapidly with Adam's hard on. Dan traced the outline of Adam's hard shaft and continued down to his full balls. He tapped several times on the cotton covered balls, causing Adam a little discomfort, but not pain. In one swift movement, he took the crop off Adam's balls and brought it down with full force on his thigh. Adam yelped, as much from surprise as pain. Dan rested the end of the crop back on his balls. "You want it as hard as that on your balls?" "No, Sir, please Sir," begged Adam. This time the 'Sir' was genuinely respectful – Adam was scared.

"First question then. Where do you keep your sex toys?" "Under the bed in the grey box," was Adam's immediate reply. Dan lifted the crop and held it horizontally in front on Adam's face. "Hold this while I go and investigate," he ordered. Adam looked puzzled. His hands were still firmly tied to the chair. Then he understood and opened his mouth for Dan to insert the bar of the crop into his mouth. "Do…not…drop..it," were Dan's last words as he headed to the bedroom. Adam looked down and saw the angry red square that the crop, now held firmly between his teeth, had left on his thigh. He tried to rationalise the situation. How could this kind of pain and humiliation be such a turn on? But, it was a turn on. The growing wet patch of precum on the pouch of the jock was irrefutable evidence. He was still staring down at his crotch when the precum was joined by dribble from his wide open mouth. He looked up, but the saliva continued to escape from the corners of his mouth and drip into his lap. He looked hopefully towards the bedroom, but there was no sign of his captor.

Eventually Dan came back with an armful of stuff and tipped it on to the dining table in front of Adam. His haul from under the bed included a leather paddle, a harness, a butt plug, 2 dildos, tit clamps, poppers and some old silk ties. Seeing all these items made Adam blush. He and Luke had played around a bit at the beginning of their relationship, usually with Adam being the Dom, but it soon died out and Adam had almost forgotten what was in the 'naughty box' under the bed.

"Quite the little perv, aren't you, boy?" observed Dan, smirking. Adam's mouth was now really aching with the effort of holding the crop and strings of spit had trailed down his chin and neck onto his hairy chest. He dare not even nod his assent for fear of sending a spray of saliva flying in Dan's direction. Dan took pity on him and removed the crop, wiping the spit onto Adam's body fur. He put it carefully on the table with the other toys.

"So, on with the interrogation," continued Dan. "You mentioned in your email before that you wanted to serve me 'not necessarily in a sexual way.' What did you mean by that?"

Adam paused. It felt much harder to confess his deepest

desires out loud in person, than to type them on a screen. Taking advantage of the pause, Dan reached for the tit clamps and attached them carefully to each of Adam's nipples. "Maybe these will jog your memory."

Adam winced and tried to take on board the pain in his nipples, before taking a deep breath and starting on his confession, "I had this fantasy about being your house boy. Cleaning up, doing your washing and ironing. Getting you food and drink when you wanted." He looked up to gauge Dan's reaction. His face was impassive, but he was listening intently. Adam plucked up his courage and carried on, "I'd like to just wear what I am wearing now while I'm working. It would be an honour for me to serve a handsome, superior stud like you, Sir."

There was a long silence as they both took in the implications of what Adam had said. Finally, Dan spoke, "and I'm assuming 'not necessarily in a sexual way' means you would like to serve me sexually too?" "Yes Sir" replied Adam without hesitation. "Just looking at you in your army gear is such a thrill for me. As you can see, it makes me hard and wet and it makes me want to do anything to please you – suck you, lick you, rim you. Have you fuck me…if you ever wanted that." He added the last phrase hastily, in case the fucking idea sounded too gay for Dan.

Dan didn't respond, but started to untie Adam's wrists and ankles from the chair. Adam was physically relieved to be able to move his stiff joints and wipe the spit from his face and neck, but mentally panicking in case he had gone too far and scared his sexy neighbour off for good. Having freed his captive, Dan took off the tit clamps one by one, causing a painful rush of blood to Adam's sore nipples. "Assume the position over the back of the sofa," he ordered. Adam obeyed and soon had his face in the seat cushion of the sofa and his exposed backside raised. He heard Dan pick something off the table and say to him, "this is for the name, rank and serial number stunt earlier." Then, without further warning, he felt a hard slap of the leather paddle across both cheeks. "Count," ordered Dan brusquely. "One Sir, thank you Sir," was Adam's obedient response. After his 10th thank you, Adam heard the paddle drop onto the carpet and saw Dan slip his army combat trousers down to his knees and threw himself onto the neighbouring armchair, legs akimbo and his hard dick jutting out from his trimmed pubes.

A finger snap from Dan and a nod to his crotch was the only order Adam needed to clamber off the sofa as fast as his enflamed ass would let him and kneel humbly in front of the dominant ex-soldier. Without having to be told, he bent down and kissed each of Dan's highly polished boots for the second time that day and said, "thank you for my punishment, Sir," before raising himself up to feast on Dan's pre-cum covered knob.

8 SERVING SARGE

Dan let Adam lick and suck the precum from his cock head for a few minutes before putting a hand firmly on his submissive neighbour's head as a signal for the blow job to begin in earnest. Even without the pressure of Dan's hand, Adam was trying his best to take the perfect, rock hard shaft down his throat. He only started to gag a little, when his lips were almost touching Dan's trimmed pubes. Dan let him up slightly to draw breath, then pushed him back down until Adam started gagging again. Three more cycles of deep-throating and a pause for breath was all it took to send the uniformed stud over the edge. As the first volley of spunk erupted in Adam's mouth, Dan pulled out and shot 2 more streams over Adam's face. He lay back again against the sofa cushions and let out a contented sigh.

Adam stayed kneeling, tasting the spunk on his tongue and feeling the rest slowly cooling on his face. Dan reached forward and wiped his own spunk off Adam's face then fed it to him. Adam sucked on the masculine, freckled fingers until they were clean again. Dan looked into his eyes and asked, "do you want to cum? "Yes please, Sir," replied Adam, eagerly. He was thrilled at the chance of getting off while Dan was still in the room as in each of their previous encounters, the ex-soldier had left or sent Adam away immediately after shooting his load.   Adam's hand was already on the soaked pouch of his jockstrap, but Dan nudged it away with his highly polished boot. Adam looked up, confused. "Beg" was Dan's one word order. "Please, Sir, I am begging you to let me cum. I am so turned on by sucking you Sir. I've never been more turned on. Please let your boy cum, Sir."

Dan paused, then slowly explained his terms for allowing the kneeling sub before him to have his release. "You have 2 minutes. You will cum on my boots. Then you will have 1 minute to lick every drop of your jizz off my size 11s." He raised his wrist, consulted the vintage Rolex and barked, "NOW!" Adam wasted no time in fishing his aching dick out of the jock and starting to wank. Despite his off-the-scale level of horniness, he was nervous and worried that he wouldn't be able to perform in time. He looked up and took in the sight of the handsome, muscled man in front of him, khaki vest showing off his shoulders to perfection and combat pants still around his thighs. His gazed swept past Dan's outheld arm, the steel bracelet of the Rolex resting on a bed of golden hair, then carried on down to the highly polished army boots. Remembering the order to cum over these symbols of Dan's power over his own, almost naked body suddenly set off Adam's orgasm and he only just had time to point the ropes of spunk exploding from his cockhead towards the leather. His orgasm was so strong that all he wanted to do was lie on the floor at Dan's feet to recover, but orders were orders and he worked his tongue hard to lick up all his own jizz within the 1 minute deadline.

Dan looked pleased. "15 seconds to spare. Good boy." With that he stood, pulled up his combats and headed towards the door. Just before letting himself out of the flat, he turned his head back and said, "My place. 7am tomorrow for your workout." "Yes, Sir" replied Adam, before sinking down onto the rug, feeling happier than he had for years.

The next morning, Adam was wide awake and hard at 6am. He was ridiculously excited that Dan had made 2 dates (not that Dan would consider them dates) so close together. He took a long shower, making sure he was squeaky clean before putting on pristine gym kit that he had even ironed the night before. He was ready to go at 6.45, but as it was a 3 minute max trip to Dan's he paced up and down his own hall until it was time to leave.

Dan, meanwhile, was still in bed, mulling things over. The interrogation scene with Adam the day before had turned him more than he expected. When he had slipped on some of his old army gear, it was more to tease poor, gay boy Adam than anything else, but he really got into it and was hard and leaking by the time he had finished paddling Adam's arse.

In the evening, horny again, he had called Kelly and after some tedious small talk about her vulnerable sister, he had persuaded her to a bit of phone sex. He wanted her to beg to suck him like Adam did, but that would never happen with Kelly. She saw blow jobs as an occasional treat that Dan should be very grateful for and the one time, early in their relationship, that he had put a bit of pressure with his hand on her head to go deeper, she had an absolute fit and told him he was a selfish lover. Over the phone, he lowered the pitch of his voice to almost a growl and told her what he'd like to do with her if they were allowed to meet up. It worked and the sound of her panting down the line, along with his right hand, made him come for a second time that day, but it wasn't nearly as intense as with Adam.

He was still thinking about this, casually stroking his morning wood, when the doorbell rang. He glanced at the clock. Adam was dead on time.

Dan threw on shorts, a vest, white gym socks and his favourite, battered old trainers and went to the front door to find a nervous Adam in his spotless kit waiting in the corridor. The 5 minutes Dan had taken to get dressed had seemed an eternity to Adam and he wondered if he had misheard the time. Dan beckoned him in and guided him to the workout area. He wasted no time in putting his slightly unfit neighbour through his paces and seemed to know just how hard to push him to get the most effort out of him. Adam's favourite bit was press ups at Dan's feet, but he only got a few brief kisses onto the old leather in between reps. The weights were the hardest as he was already knackered from the cardio, but the sight of Dan's biceps working hard with far heavier weights than his own, spurred him on.

Adam was a sweaty mess by the time Dan decided the workout was over and when he was ordered to run to the kitchen to get water, it was definitely more of a walk. He handed Dan one glass and took several big swigs from his own. Dan was wiping the sweat from his face with a small towel. Adam had no such luxury and had to use the edge of his T-shirt to get the salt water from his forehead.

As soon as he got his breath back, Dan nodded slightly to the mat and Adam immediately knelt on the spot Dan had indicated. Towering above him, Dan kicked off his trainers and lowered his shorts, revealing his beautiful hard cock. Adam licked his lips expectantly and leaned towards the glistening cockhead of his army master. Dan shook his head and said, "balls." The momentary disappointment at not being allowed to taste Dan's knob disappeared when Adam's tongue made contact with Dan's shaved and very sweaty balls. They tasted kind of nutty and so masculine. Adam covered every square centimetre with his eager tongue while Dan wanked slowly above his head. Adam felt Dan's balls rise up and then heard a guttural roar as he came. He felt the hot spunk land on his head, then face and finally his T-shirt.

To Adam's surprise, Dan whipped off his vest, wiped the remaining cum from his cock, took off his socks and piled the soiled kit in front of Adam. "Those are to be back to me here at midday tomorrow, washed and ironed," he said before heading off towards the bathroom. Adam stared lustfully at his muscled back and beautifully proportioned, rock hard buns as he retreated across the room. He scooped up the sweaty, spunk-soaked kit and headed, blushing, into the corridor, praying that he didn't meet any other neighbours.

9 PAIN AND PLEASURE

Adam managed to get back to his flat with the sweaty, spunky pile of gym kit without being spotted. He was about to head straight to the laundry room, but now he was back in the privacy of his own home, the temptation to sniff Dan's shorts and socks grew too powerful. He diverted to his bedroom, lay on the bed and carefully brought each item up to his nose with his left hand whilst wanking his aching dick with his right. It was a sock that did it – sweaty, but not rank, exuding Dan's masculine scent. He ejaculated over his own face and the sock, then drifted off to a blissful sleep, exhausted after the intense work out and the excitement of another amazing encounter with Dan.

When he woke an hour later, the reality of the situation hit him. Here he was laying on his bed, surrounded by an ex-soldier's used gym kit and feeling as if he had won the lottery and was sleeping on a pile of £20 notes. How could he explain to anyone - even his gay friends – how happy it made him to serve and worship this powerful, straight man? He started thinking about the future and how, the more obsessed he got with Dan, the more likely it was to end in heartbreak when lockdown ended and the pert, blond Kelly was back on the scene. Then he decided it was worth it. He had nothing else to do and he had never been so turned on by anyone, so fuck it, while Dan still wanted him around, he was damn well going to be there for him.

With that, he stripped off his own gym kit and put everything in the washer, actually getting a little hard again at the thought of being Dan's servant.

At 11.59 the next day, Adam was at Dan's front door, holding the clean laundry in his arms. He rang the bell at midday precisely and a few moments later, his neighbour opened the door, mobile phone in hand and gestured Adam to come in. Dan continued his phone conversation, clearly with someone on the end of the line who was not best pleased. Dan flung himself on the sofa next to an open laptop and gestured to his bare feet. Adam interpreted correctly that this was a sign to start giving the harassed security expert a calming foot massage. He was only too willing to oblige, so set the ironed gym kit carefully down on the coffee table and knelt at Dan's feet to begin work. He heard Dan make some more conciliatory remarks and then say, "could you put him on the line please?" To Adam's surprise, Dan suddenly switched to French and not very polite French at that. Adam picked out 'conard' and 'sac de merde' amongst other choice insults. Dan was fluent, but somehow his slightly cockney English accent found its way into his French one. 'As if this guy couldn't get any more sexy' thought Adam as he continued to massage his hero's beautiful size 11 feet.

The phone call ended abruptly with a "ça suffit" from Dan and his hurling the phone across the room. He glared down at Adam and said "you are supposed to be in a jockstrap only when you are working on my feet." Adam recalled the rules Dan had issued in his flat – he had written them down after their meeting and knew them off by heart. They didn't include wearing a jockstrap during foot worship, but Dan did not look like he was in a mood to be argued with, so Adam just mumbled, "sorry Sir." Ignoring the apology, Dan ordered "strip and get over that coffee table." To Adam's dismay, Dan swiped the whole pile of carefully ironed laundry off the table onto the floor before marching out of the room. He hurried to obey the order and by the time Dan came back with a very solid looking army belt, he was already bent over the table, naked ass in the air. Dan didn't hold back, using all the strength in his powerful right arm to lay into Adam with the heavy belt. By the 7th stroke, Adam was yelping and begging for mercy. "Shut up and take it like a man," was Dan's pitiless response as he laid on more hard strokes. Finally, he threw the belt on the floor and ordered a very sore Adam off the table and onto the floor to kiss his tormentor's feet. As soon as he started kissing, Dan felt moisture on the bridge of his foot and realised Adam was crying. This, combined with the livid red marks he saw on Adam's upturned arse, made the last vestiges of his rage ebb away and he bent down to gently raise his prostrate neighbour's head with a hand under his chin. Adam's big, brown eyes, still moist with tears, looked up at him with a mixture of fear and love. Dan led him to the sofa and patted the seat next to him. Adam sat down very slowly - even the soft sofa cushions sent renewed waves of pain across his well punished backside.

Dan put his arm over Adam's bare shoulders and despite

the pain, the touch of it sent an electric current of pleasure through him. "You did say I could take work frustrations out on you," said Dan. Adam nodded silently. "Tell me," ventured Dan in a concerned voice. Adam spoke quietly: "I'm not going back on my offer, but that was a really hard thrashing. You were drunk last time you belted me and I didn't realise your sober strength. That fucking hurt." Dan laughed, which broke the tension and made Adam laugh too. "I guess I did go a bit hard on you, but that silly French bastard has caused a big problem with a billionaire client – it was him I wanted to beat really." He gave Adam's shoulder a reassuring squeeze. "Tell you what, I'll let you choose what we do now…within reason."

Adam hesitated then just came out with it, "well, I saw this dom guy a couple of times – a school teacher. He used to work out his frustration at cheeky pupils on me with a belt or cane, then he used to have me kiss his ass – to give him pleasure where he had given me pain." He glanced around at Dan to gauge wether his idea was 'within reason.' Dan was smiling. "Give me pleasure where I've given you pain. I like it." He withdrew his arm from Adam's shoulder's, pulled his grey joggers down to his ankles and draped himself over the back of the sofa. Adam began with very gentle kisses at the crease between Dan's thighs and arse cheeks, then slowly worked his way all round each cheek. From the contented sighs and muttered 'good boys' Dan was clearly enjoying this new experience, so Adam decided to risk taking things up a notch by poking his warm tongue into Dan's crack. "Jesus fuuuuuck," exclaimed Dan, "so that's what rimming feels like. It's amazing." Encouraged, Adam very gently parted Dan's cheeks with his hands, revealing a smattering of blond hair and a twitching pink hole which he licked intently. Dan was now groaning constantly and pushed back into Adam's face so that he had enough room to reach his leaking cock and start wanking. "I'm gonna cum," he shouted. "Get on it." Adam stopped licking and swung himself under Dan's stomach and got his knob in his mouth just in time to swallow a huge load of soldier spunk.

Dan lay back on the sofa, panting and Adam hitched himself up to sit beside him. His own dick was hard as a rock, but, conscious of his still painfully throbbing arse against the leather of the sofa, thought he had better not risk more punishment by wanking in front of Dan without his permission. Coming out of his post-coital daze, Dan noticed his neighbour's desperate erection and took pity on him. "OK, you can cum, but you make sure you catch it in your hand. I don't want your jizz on my sofa." "Thank you, Sir," replied Adam in a very grateful tone.

10 A MASTER'S KISS

Adam let himself back into his flat and headed straight for the sofa. He eased himself down gently as his arse was still very tender from Dan's hard belting and his head was still spinning a little. He could taste the remnants of his own and Dan's cum in his mouth and felt used, slutty and very content. The thought that he had really pleased his military master and the tenderness he showed after the beating made Adam feel as warm on the inside as his ass was on the outside. Dan had made their next appointment for Friday morning. Another training session. The thought of the muscled stud putting him through his paces made him hard again.

Friday seemed to come around very slowly and once again Adam was pacing up and down his hall 15 minutes early in his pristine gym kit, waiting for the appointed hour.

In retrospect, he wished he had been able to sleep in a bit later to save his energy. Dan put him through a tough cardio and weights session and then announced they were going for a run. Adam tried to protest, but a firm arm on his back propelled him out of the flat. The path they took, across the Thames via Wandsworth Bridge and back over Battersea Bridge would normally have been a picturesque route taking in the London skyline, but Adam was having to concentrate on staying upright, rather than admiring the view. Dan had to keep stopping to encourage him and finally they made it back to the riverside walk near their apartment building.

"So, just to make it interesting, we'll race the last 100 metres to the front door. Every 10 seconds you are behind me, means 1 stroke on your backside. GO!"

Dan raced off, leaving the exhausted Adam way behind and it seemed an eternity before he slumped towards the grinning Dan, whose eyes were fixed on his watch. "55 seconds behind. We'll call it 6 strokes – can't give you half a one, can I?"

Adam was too breathless to reply, so just trailed miserably behind his ruthless trainer into the lobby. Once inside Dan's flat, Adam slid down the wall to sit on the floor, not an ounce of energy left. Dan brought them both large glasses of tap water and gave his protegé just enough time for his breathing to get back to some sort of regularity before announcing, "Might as well get the forfeit over. Get those shorts off and assume the position over the dining table." The tingle of excitement that Adam would normally have felt at receiving such an order from Dan did not appear as his body was so sweaty and aching, but he slowly obeyed as Dan headed to his bedroom. He slipped his shorts off and wondered about the jockstrap underneath. Dan had only mentioned his shorts, so he kept the jock on and bent over the dining table, arms stretched out in front of him. He turned his head and saw Dan striding across the room, a riding crop in his hand.

As Dan approached, he saw Adam's exposed ass framed by the white straps of his jock. There were traces of bruising from the belting he had delivered 2 days before.

This sight evoked mixed reactions in Dan. His cock hardened in his shorts at the power he had over this willing, obedient guy, but he did feel a bit guilty about the bruising. Not guilty enough to dispense with the cropping though. It was part of the training to ensure that Adam gave his 100% commitment. After 3 relatively hard strokes, Adam was already crying – not so much from the pain, but more the exhaustion and sense of unfairness that he had pushed himself so hard and was still being punished.

Dan went easier on the last 3 strokes, put down the crop and lent down to speak quietly in Adam's ear: "It's OK, babe. You worked hard and you'll see the results in your body really soon. I'm proud of you, but I need to maintain discipline to keep you motivated."

The 'babe' made all the difference. It was what Dan called Kelly and – in Adam's mind at least – meant that he did have some feelings for Adam too. Suddenly the exhaustion, aching limbs and striped arse all seemed worth it and the tears stopped immediately.

"Come on," announced Dan. "Plenty of room in the shower for 2. You can soap my back." Adam did not need telling twice and followed Dan to the bathroom seconds later. The sight of a naked Dan already under the water was enough to make Adam weak at his already shaky knees and he had to prop himself against the tiled wall to take off the rest of his kit." He stepped into the large walk-in shower and started with the soap on Dan's perfectly proportioned back. He worked his way down his neighbour's meaty arse cheeks, then the muscular thighs coated with fine blond hair and down to his ankles, before Dan turned around to face the crouching Adam and lifted one foot after the other for a thorough cleansing. He worked his way back up to Dan's cock and balls, gently pulling back the generous foreskin to ensure no centimetre of skin was left untouched. He stood back up to concentrate on Dan's perfect pecs and swooshed the soap round through his chest hair until Dan took Adam's hand in his, put it gently to his side and leant in for a kiss.

Before Adam knew what was happening, Dan had shut off the water and was leading him out of the shower. "Dry me," he whispered, handing Adam a warm fluffy towel from the heated rail. Adam followed the same pattern as in the shower and started at his army stud's shoulders, working his way down the back of his body, then up from the feet at the front. The very gentle rubbing of the towel against his heavy balls was too much for Dan and he kept Adam down on his knees, for a long, luxuriant blow job. His load felt smaller than usual in Adam's mouth when he eventually came – he was still a bit dehydrated from the run – but the taste was intense and addictive for his infatuated neighbour. He started to shiver, realising he had been so busy tending to Dan, that he had not dried himself. Dan picked another warm towel from the rail and put it round Adam's shoulders. He left him to get dry and headed to the bedroom.

By the time Adam joined him, Dan was dressed in chinos and a button down blue shirt. He nodded to a grey track suit on the bed and said, "you can borrow that – save putting your sweaty gear back on." Adam thanked him, touched by the macho man's thoughtfulness. "It's OK.

You can bring it back tomorrow once you've washed it with the gym kit and towels."

It was clear that the brief romantic interlude was over and Adam was back to being the gay slave boy to his straight, military master. The tent of his hard cock in the borrowed tracksuit bottoms suggested that he didn't mind this too much and with a respectful "Yes, Sir" he took his leave to pick up the damp towels and gym kit from the bathroom floor.

11 SHAVED AND FUCKED

Dan went to his desk, very relaxed after Adam's devoted ministrations, and started going through his emails. The French disaster had been resolved and his English clients needed very little protection at the moment as they were either sitting out Covid on their yachts or in their country estates. His mind wandered back to this morning's events and in particular the kiss in the shower. It had been a spur of the moment thing. Adam had looked so adoringly up at him whilst soaping his chest that he felt a rush of affection. He remembered his freak out the week before at the thought he might be turning gay and now, here he was instigating intimacy with a bloke. His no-nonsense working class upbringing and years of army life had not equipped Dan with many tools for introspection, so after dwelling a bit more on this kiss, he thought, fuck it – it felt good – why not?

He spent the afternoon calling round his team members who were on furlough and FaceTime'd Kelly. She wasn't in a very chatty mood as being cooped up with her sister for week on end wasn't her idea of fun. Dan tried to make a joke about it, but she would not be cheered. By 5pm he was bored and restless. He checked Netlix and saw that one of the Marvel films had been released. He wished there was someone to watch it with. Then he thought, actually there is.

Adam saw the text from an unknown number; another scam no doubt, so ignored it until he had finished the chapter of the novel he was reading. En route to the kitchen to make tea, he checked the message, just in case. It read, "Do you fancy coming round for a film & pizza? You're allowed the calories after this morning's work out LOL." Adam then realised it was from Dan. The number was unknown as Dan had never giving him his number, in case of 'pestering' as he had put it. Then he panicked. He had ignored the text for over half an hour. Would the offer still be open? He typed "Yes please Sir" as fast as he could. Thoughts of tea were forgotten as he stared at his phone, willing Dan to reply quickly. 5 minutes later another text appeared "Great. No need for the Sir tonight. See you 7ish"

Adam was still in the tracksuit Dan had lent him and although he was loath to take it off, he decided it wasn't appropriate for movie night with his sexy neighbour. As he tried on various outfits, he had to remind himself that it wasn't a date. Just neighbours watching a film, right? Because lockdown prevented them from seeing their friends and loved ones. In the end he opted for an outfit he definitely would have worn on a date – black jeans, fitted white shirt, Gucci belt, invisible socks and black suede loafers. A white jockstrap underneath.

As usual, despite a long and thorough shower, he was ready too early and so poured himself a large vodka and tonic to calm the nerves before heading down to Dan's.

He rang the door at precisely 7 and Dan greeted him in the same button-down shirt and chinos that he was wearing earlier. Adam smiled to himself – clearly wardrobe panic was an unknown phenomenon to ex-Sergeant Russell. After fishing out a smaller bag to keep for himself, he handed over a carrier of booze. "I wasn't sure what you liked with your pizza," he ventured. "Depends who I'm with," replied Dan. "Red wine if I'm with a posh boy like you, beers if it's with the army mates." Adam laughed, "I brought you both, just in case."

Adam followed Dan through and took a seat at the kitchen island. He spotted a recently opened can of lager, the condensation from the fridge still running down its sides and an opened, but untouched bottle of Pauillac Bordeax. "That's a bit fancy for pizza night isn't it?" he asked, noting the 2016 vintage.

"I have contacts in Bordeaux. In fact, my ex-wife and daughter live there. A friend shipped some over for me to help me get through lockdown and I've had no one to share it with."

Adam was no longer so interested in the wine. He didn't know Dan had been married, let alone that he was a dad. He realised that in their handful of meetings, the only conversation had been about working out and then sex.

Two hours later they were still talking, swapping life histories, the delivered pizza demolished along with the bottle of fine red wine and all thoughts of the movie forgotten. "Why did you get divorced?" asked Adam. "She's a beautiful woman from a very wealthy family. At first she liked this rough diamond English soldier, but as you may have noticed, I like to be in charge and she wasn't too keen on taking orders. I wanted to come back to London, but she flatly refused. It kills me not seeing my daughter. She's 12 now, but between her mother being awkward and Kelly not exactly being great step-mother material, I only get to see her 3 or 4 times a year." Dan trailed off, the sadness clearly visible in his eyes.

Adam got up from his stool and went to the other side of the island to put his arms round Dan's shoulders. To his surprise, Dan swivelled on his barstool to take Adam's face in his hands and kissed him passionately on the lips. Eventually he pulled back, his hands still on Adam's face. "I think I want to fuck you," he announced quietly. Adam nodded, his heart pounding. This ex-soldier was certainly a master of the surprise manoeuvre. "First though, we need to deal with that hairy arse of yours. I don't mind this," he continued, unbuttoning Adam's shirt and running his fingers through the chest hair, "but I like my pussies smooth." His tone changed from seductive to authoritative in an instant. "Strip and bend over the island,"

He left the room and Adam wasted no time in tearing off his carefully chosen outfit. The marble felt cold against his bare chest as he leant over it, legs spread and arse exposed. Dan soon returned with a cut throat razor in one hand and a can of shaving cream in the other. "Are you sure your hand is steady enough for this after all that beer and wine?" asked Adam teasingly. Dan put the razor and the can down on the counter and held out his strong hands with perfect stillness in front of Adam's face. "Army training," he laughed and slapped Adam's right ass cheek with full force, "so don't question me, boy." "Yes, Sir. Sorry, Sir," replied Adam, reaching back to pull his cheeks apart.

Within a few minutes and a dozen expert strokes of the blade, Adam's ass was smooth as a baby's. Dan slapped the left cheek this time and ordered, "get into the shower to wash this off. Then get to the bedroom and prepare yourself. I assume that little bag you left by the front door contains the necessary?" Adam blushed. He had not expected Dan to even notice, but the bag did indeed contain a small bottle of lube and some condoms. "Busted," he thought to himself. He raised himself slowly off the counter and turned to face Dan, who had an inscrutable expression on his face. "Dan...Sir..." he began falteringly, "I haven't been fucked for ages. I was the top with Luke and you're so big...um, please will you take it easy with me?"

Dan's expression didn't change. "We'll see. Now get moving before I take my belt to you."

15 minutes later Dan entered his bedroom to find a naked, lubed Adam on all fours on his bed. "Mmmm. Keen I see," he remarked. "Come over here and undress me. Adam crawled backwards off the bed and went over to Dan. He slowly unbuttoned the blue cotton shirt, kissing the muscled chest being revealed as he did so. He took the shirt off and placed it carefully on a chair before kneeling before Dan and unbuckling his belt. Dan lifted one bare foot at a time to allow his desperate neighbour to take his chinos off, then pulled his head into the white cotton of his briefs. Adam licked at the cotton until the veiny shaft

became visible through the wet fabric. Eventually Dan gave the signal to take down his briefs and Adam dived on to his exposed dick like a starving man.

After 10 minutes of expert head, Dan worried that he might cum too soon, so pulled Adam off by the hair and handed him the lube. Adam massaged lube carefully up and down Dan's shaft and over his cockhead until his military stud was satisfied and nodded back towards the bed. Adam took up his previous position on all fours and soon felt Dan's hard-on against his hole. Dan slowly rubbed his lubed dick up and down his crack and reached forward to push the fingers of his other hand into Dan's mouth. "You know where these are going next, boy," he growled as Adam sucked them with a vengeance, trying to get as much saliva on them as possible. Dan pulled out his fingers and inserted them one at a time into Adam's asshole.

Soon Adam was panting and moaning, pushing back on Dan's fingers. Dan slowly, slowly pulled out his fingers and lined up his knob. "You can do this, baby boy. Take Sarge's dick. Make him happy." Adam wasn't sure whether it was the 'baby boy' or the 'Sarge's dick' that did it, but his sphincter suddenly relaxed and Dan's cockhead entered him. Dan pushed on in, millimetre by millimetre, encouraging Adam with lots of 'good boys'

Finally, Adam felt Dan's trimmed pubes against his newly shaven hole. Dan stayed very still, allowing his neighbour to acclimatise to being filled with a big soldier's cock, before slowly starting to ease in and out. Gradually he built up the pace and the encouraging 'good boys' were replaced with 'gay boys' and 'sluts.'

As Dan sped up the fuck, Adam started wanking himself, whispering repeatedly, "You're the Master. You're the Master." "Yes I fucking am your Master, shouted just before he came, unloading a hot fountain of spunk into Adam, who in turn shot violently into the mattress beneath him.

12 ADAM REBELS

Dan pulled slowly out of Adam with a contented sigh and rolled onto his back. Adam, still on all fours, looked down at the pool of his sperm that was sinking into Dan's sheets. "I'm so sorry Sir, I'll clean it up before I go." Dan glanced over at the sheet and laughed. "Fucked a big load out of ya, didn't I?" Adam nodded, blushing. "Clean it up, but you don't have to go. Stay with me tonight." Adam cracked a huge smile at the totally unexpected invitation and rushed to the bathroom to get towels before Dan changed his mind.

When he came back in, Dan was looking pensive. "Should I have worn one of these?" he asked, holding up a condom from the little bag Adam had left on the bedside table with the lube. He blushed again. "Um, well I'm on prep, so it's OK." "What's prep?" asked Dan. Adam nearly laughed, but remembered the last time he had mocked Dan's lack of knowledge of the gay world had earned him a belting. "It's an anti-HIV drug. It protects us both," he replied with a serious tone. Good," said Dan, "It felt really good without." "For me too," was Adam's understated reply. "Shall I clean you up?" he continued, holding up a face cloth soaked in warm water. Dan grinned. "That is what I call good service."

Adam lovingly wiped the lube and spunk from his military hunk's cock and balls, carefully retracting the foreskin to ensure a thorough clean. "It's kind of in my own interest, Sir, in case you wake up in the morning wanting a blow job." Dan smiled and nodded as he thought about Adam's confession. "You would have sucked it uncleaned though - if I'd ordered you to – wouldn't you boy?" "Yes Sir," was Adam's honest reply.

He cleaned up his own spunk as best he could with a dry towel and slipped back into bed with Dan, barely believing his luck. When Dan turned off the light and turned to spoon him, Adam's happiness was complete.

Dan woke early and was surprised to feel a hairy chest brushing against his arm. After a few seconds, he realised it was Adam. He withdrew his arm and rolled onto his back. What had he been thinking? The sex was great, but he shouldn't have let Adam stay. It felt more like being unfaithful to Kelly than a quick blow job or foot massage had done. He was about to nudge Adam and tell him to go home when the handsome neighbour woke up by himself. In his sleepy first view of Dan's chiselled face, he didn't recognise the troubled expression and dived straight in with a cheery "good morning Sir, ready for that blow job?"

Dan realised that despite his guilty thoughts, he was hard and pulled back the duvet to let Adam do his expert work. His alternation between loving ball licking and deep throating his neighbour's shaft soon had Dan coming in his mouth with a deep grunt. Adam swallowed it all down like a good boy and then carefully licked Dan's knob clean. He lay back and took hold of his own cock. Dan pulled at his arm, "oh no you don't. Not after the mess you made on my bed. You don't get to cum until those sheets are laundered and ironed and put back on." "Yes Sir," replied Adam, ruefully contemplating his aching hardon.

Dan got out of bed and strode towards the kitchen. "Bring back the bedding this evening," was his only farewell.

Adam got dressed, stripped the bed and headed back to his own flat, his hardon still uncomfortable in his trousers. As soon as he arrived home, he put Dan's soiled sheets and towels straight into the washing machine and for some reason this act made him even hornier. It felt really slavey to be acting as a house boy for a masculine stud and being ordered not to cum as a punishment for spilling his seed in his master's bed seemed perfectly reasonable. His shower was a trial as the soaping of his cock and balls nearly sent him over the edge. He turned the water cold and got out when his erection had subsided.

At lunchtime he was watching the television news whilst ironing Dan's sheets. Unlike 90% of the country, his heart sank when he heard the headline that the prime minister was to announce a phased end to most lockdown restrictions in 3 weeks time. While everyone else was jumping for joy at getting their normal lives back, all Adam could think of was that Dan would be back with Kelly and would have no further use for his male neighbour.

At just before 7, he rang Dan's doorbell, neat pile of linen in one hand. Dan opened the door, smiling. "Good boy," he beamed, seeing the result of Adam's hard work. "Go and make the bed back up and join me in the kitchen."

Adam made the bed as neatly as he could, pausing to sniff the pillows for a hint of Dan's scent as he put the clean covers back on, then went through to the kitchen where Dan was sitting at the counter watching the prime minister giving opening up details on the TV. He pushed a glass of chilled white Burgundy towards Adam, who took a grateful sip.

"Kelly's already been on the phone," he began without preamble. "She wants to move in full time when it's allowed next month."

"That's nice for you," replied Adam, unsuccessfully attempting a smile. "Don't worry, we can still see each other until then. In fact, it got a bit saucy with Kelly on the phone and I need sorting out. On your knees, boy!"

The normally obedient Adam snapped. "I don't want to be fucking Kelly's sloppy seconds," he shouted and turned to leave. He had only taken 2 steps before Dan was right by him and had his angry neighbour's arm twisted painfully behind his back. "You, boy, are not going anywhere until I tell you to," he whispered menacingly into Adam's ear. Dan's proximity and the hypnotising power of his voice melted away Adam's anger instantly. Dan released his arm. "Strip," he ordered, still in a whisper. Adam obeyed. When he got down to his jockstrap, Dan told him to assume the position over the back of the sofa and went to fetch his riding crop.

Six hard, parallel strokes taught a contrite Adam not to provoke the ex-soldier and the stripes that took almost a week to fade, drove home the lesson. Adam was still draped over the sofa when he heard rustling behind him and he flinched as the buckle of Dan's belt touched his bruised ass. He cried out as Dan's firm hands rekindled the pain when they spread his cheeks apart. He heard Dan spit, then felt a warm wad on his hole. Dan pushed his rock hard cock in without much mercy, showing none of the tenderness of last night's love making. Adam yelled out, but his mouth was soon covered by Dan's left hand. He continued to fuck hard and fast until he roared out and Adam felt the pulsing of cum inside him. Dan pulled out and helped Adam to stand. "Clean me up like you did last night," he ordered and Adam hobbled gingerly to the bathroom for towels, Dan's spunk leaking out of his battered hole as he crossed the room.

He quickly wiped himself as best he could, not wanting to keep Dan waiting. When he got back into the living room, Dan was on the sofa, legs spread and arms behind his head like a triumphant warrior. Adam knelt between his muscular legs and gently wiped his master's cock and balls with a damp cloth.

"I'm sorry for being rude, Sir,' he apologized meekly when he had finished and carefully tucked Dan's cock and balls back into his jeans.

"I was going to let you cum tonight as well," said Dan in a rueful voice as if it were his own aching hard on in question.

Adam did not reply, but knelt further down to kiss each of Dan's bare feet in subjugation.

13 REWARD FOR GOOD BEHAVIOUR

To Adam's surprise, Dan patted the sofa next to him, indicating that his well-punished neighbour should hop up and join him. As Adam sat down, he winced. Dan had not held back with the crop. "How did you come to have a crop anyway?" he asked fidgeting on his seat. "I'm not as uncouth as you think, posh boy. My uncle bred horses, but he sold off the stud years ago and I got out of the habit of riding. I remembered I had the kit, though, at the back of the wardrobe," explained Dan.

Adam's neglected cock twitched again at the thought of Dan's sculpted body contained in riding gear. "Don't suppose you have boots and jodhpurs do you?" asked Adam hopefully. "Yep," grinned Dan, stroking his hand along the bar of the crop he had just used so expertly on Adam's rump.

"Please will you wear them one day for me Sir?" asked Adam in a pleading tone.

"If you are a very good boy," replied Dan slowly

Dan switched on the TV and lined up a detective series he was half way through. Adam was not consulted on the viewing options, but despite his still sore ass, was delighted to just be with Dan on the sofa like a regular couple.

Adam ended up staying the night again and woke up to Dan spooning him, hard on lined up with his still tender arse crack. He was torn – did he keep still and relish the feeling of the man of his dreams cuddling him for a little while longer or give into the temptation of diving down to his neighbours inviting morning wood? After 5 minutes, romance lost out to lust and Adam carefully positioned himself lower down the bed and began to gently kiss and lick Dan's veined shaft. It wasn't long before his ministrations woke Dan and Adam felt a firm hand on his head, guiding him to the ex-soldiers leaking knob. Without warning, Dan started to piston in and out of Adam's mouth, causing him to gag, but he did not pull away until he felt a hot fountain of spunk fill his mouth and go up his nose. He was finally allowed to pull off, spluttering and coughing. "It's your own fault, buddy," laughed Dan, "you started it."

With that, he leapt out of bed and headed to the ensuite. Adam listened to the strong flow of piss hitting the toilet bowl and wondered what the mixture of sperm and urine would taste like if he were to lick the remnants off Dan's knob. The thought made his already aching dick even harder and he clenched his fists into the bedsheet to prevent himself touching his boner without permission.

A naked Dan strode back into the bedroom and clicked his fingers, motioning to the floor in front of him. Adam jumped out of bed, his rock hard cock swinging in front of him and knelt before Dan.

Dan looked down with a serious expression.

"You were disobedient and rude last night, weren't you, boy?" Adam looked up with regret. "Yes, Sir. Very rude Sir."

"And that meant I had to whip you and not let you cum, didn't it, boy?"

"Yes Sir," replied Adam, fidgeting as Dan's reference to last night's whipping with the riding crop reminded him that his bruised buttocks were resting on his heels as he knelt.

"However, you've been a good boy this morning, so you are allowed to wank." As he said this, Dan adjusted his stance so that his 2 bare feet were pressed against each other. "Here's your target. DO NOT mess up my carpet."

Adam understood immediately, grabbed his shaft and started tugging furiously on it. Seconds later 2 arcs of spunk landed on the bridges of Dan's feet. Adam, still panting from the intensity of his orgasm, bent down and licked every drop off Dan's salty flesh.

"Thank you Sir," he said quietly, not sure which he was more grateful for – the bliss of being allowed to cum, or the taste of his own spunk mingling with Dan's on his tongue. "I love you Sir," he whispered without looking up, not being able to help himself, but thinking he had spoken too softly for Dan to hear.

Dan reached down to help a slightly woozy Adam to his

feet. "Come and help me in the shower?" he asked – an invitation, not an order. "That would be a great pleasure Sir," replied Adam with mock formality, grinning from ear to ear.

In the shower, Adam lovingly soaped Dan's muscular back, then crouched down to clean his smooth, white buttocks, gently parting them to run a soapy hand down his crack. Dan's moans were audible at this point, even above the rush of the water. Adam carried on down the backs of Dan's blond-haired legs and with a gentle pressure on his calf, gestured his military Master to turn round.

Once Dan was facing him, Adam set to work on soaping the feet he had so recently licked clean of his own spunk, then worked his way slowly up to the cock and balls he was so obsessed with. He cleaned Dan's equipment with utmost care, causing the flaccid cock to swell a little. He finished by soaping and massaging Dan's firm pecs. To his surprise, Dan took the bottle of body wash from his hand and started to return the favour. Although his cleaning of Adam's hairy body was a little more brisk than his boy's reverent service, he did soap every part of Adam, bruised buttocks included. By the time Dan rested the bottle back on the shower shelf, Adam was weak at the knees from the prolonged attention from his Master and had to reach out to the tiled wall for support as Dan turned off the water.

They stepped out and Adam dried Dan with a fluffy towel, still warm from the heated rack. Dan stood still, legs spread and feet firmly planted on the tiled floor and allowed Adam to work, a contented look on his face as if it were perfectly normal to have a personal body slave at your disposal. This time the favour was not returned and, as Dan went through to the bedroom to dress, Adam was forced to use the now damp towel on himself. After the intense pleasure of the shower, it was, however, a small price to pay.

He lingered in the bathroom for a while, savouring the moment and trying to keep the thought from his mind that Kelly would be moving in to replace him in a few weeks. By the time he threw on some clothes and wandered through to the kitchen, Dan was rustling up scrambled eggs whilst humming 'Moonlight Serenade.' Adam quietly fell in love a little bit more.

14 RIDING MASTER

Dan was lost in his thoughts as he whipped up scrambled eggs. He couldn't remember when he had been so contented. When he first started seeing Adam, the bizarreness of the situation prayed on his mind and he worried constantly that someone would find out he was having sex with a guy. Now it didn't seem normal exactly, but it didn't freak him out and he liked having Adam around. He couldn't help comparing Adam to his girlfriend, Kelly and apart from the look and feel of her pert breasts, that he still missed, Adam usually came out top in any comparison. Just as he was thinking this, Dan sensed something behind him and looked over his shoulder to see Adam, staring at him adoringly with his big brown eyes. It looked like Adam had been standing there for a while and it crossed his mind that Kelly would never stand there, just gazing at him.

Dan smiled at Adam, who had borrowed a pair of grey shorts, that were too big for him and hung low around his hips. His dark chest hair was still a bit damp as he had dried off somewhat ineffectively with Dan's used towel. "Sit," said Dan, waving an eggy wooden spoon towards a barstool at the kitchen counter. He saw Adam wince as his tender buttocks touched the hard plastic of the stool. The thought that Adam was still feeling the beating he had given him the night before for shouting about Kelly made Dan's cock twitch. He loved the power he had over his handsome, younger neighbour. His cock twitched again when Adam said "Thank you, sir' as Dan placed his breakfast on the counter in front of him. He noticed that Adam did not pick up his own knife and fork until Dan was seated beside him and had had his first mouthful of the perfectly cooked eggs.

They ate in companionable silence. Dan was thinking about the mumbled 'I love you' that he thought he had heard from Adam just after he had licked his own jizz off Dan's feet. Even a few days ago, that would have set off alarm bells in his head. All his fears about the sensitive gay neighbour taking their relationship much too seriously would have kicked in and Dan would have finished the whole thing immediately. Today, however, he didn't mind this declaration of love, in fact it made him realise how much he liked Adam. He struck while the iron was hot and said, without preamble, "Would you like to stay here full time with me until you-know-who moves in when Lockdown ends?" Adam's eyes widened in disbelief. He stuttered "Yes please Sir" and Dan engulfed him in vice-like hug.

Once Adam had cleaned the kitchen, which took a while as Dan was not a tidy cook, he wandered over to the desk where Dan was reading emails. Dan took advantage of the loose fit of Adam's borrowed shorts and slipped his hand under the waistband to cup his boy's buttock. "You'd better go and pack some clothes that fit, otherwise I'll be groping you all day long." Adam thought to himself that that would not be a problem for him, but just smiled and said, "Yes Sir, right away."

Back in his flat, Adam agonised about which items of his wardrobe would please dominant neighbour most and made sure to include all his underwear from sedate cotton boxers to skimpy jockstraps, to cater for any whim Dan might have. An hour later he was back at Dan's front door, baggage in tow.

Adam had not been the only one busy in the wardrobe and when Dan opened the front door, Adam's eyes nearly popped out of his head when he saw the 6'2" stud dressed in a pristine white polo shirt and tight cream jodhpurs tucked into black leather riding boots. Adam actually tripped over the threshold in his excitement to get in and had to be caught in the strong, golden-haired arms of his neighbour. Dan laughed briefly, then changed to a sterner tone. "Strip to your underwear here before you follow me into the living room." he ordered, before turning on his heal to leave the hallway. Adam did not obey immediately as he was transfixed by Dan's meaty arse, perfectly encased in the tight jodhpurs, but he was nevertheless in the living room, stripped to his white jockstrap in less than a minute. Dan was standing, legs apart, holding a riding crop in his right hand. Dan said nothing, but nodded his approval at Adam's underwear choice and used the crop to gesture to the floor directly in front of him. Adam understood the unspoken order and knelt before his master. He looked briefly up at Dan, but was told, "eyes on the boots". Adam lowered his gaze immediately. Dan continued, "they are a bit dusty. They've been in the back of the wardrobe for years. I was going to give them a wipe, but then I remembered I had an eager slave boy for that. The shoe kit is in the hall cupboard. Get to it!" Adam stood a little shakily and headed for the hall. He returned with the shoeshine kit, knelt once again and started to gently wipe the dust off the black leather.

Knowing how much Adam adored worshipping his bare feet, Dan had planned to have him give the boots a cursory wipe, maybe a kiss or two and then allow him to take them off, but the feeling of Adam's hands through the leather was much more pleasurable than he had expected. "I think they need some polish too, don't you, boy?" he said, whilst stroking the riding crop gently over Adam's bare shoulders and back. He sat down to make himself comfortable while his boy spread out a sheet newspaper and gently lifted one boot at a time onto it, before carefully unfastening the tin of polish and then brushing it into the dry leather. Adam was intent on his task and continued to obey the 'eyes on the boots' order whilst diligently polishing and buffing. He did not see the huge grin of contentment on Dan's face as he enjoyed the boot blacking. Eventually, the boots were shined to Dan's satisfaction, and he signalled this to Adam by raising his head with the crop under his chin. As he raised him up to a higher kneeling position, Dan noticed a large wet spot at the front of Adam's tented jockstrap. "'You enjoyed that, boy, didn't you?" "Yes Master, I loved polishing your boots. I am so grateful, Master" replied Adam without hesitation. It was the first time he had called Dan 'Master' directly and it made both their cocks twitch even harder. "You'd better show me how grateful," whispered Dan, brushing the end of his crop along the gleaming leather. Adam got back down and smothered each boot in turn with ardent kisses.

Dan had planned a longer session, but the passionate kisses on his riding boots was just one stimulus too far the aching cock that felt like it was trying to drill out of his jodhpurs. "Go and get the lube", he ordered. Minutes later, Adam was bent over the back of the sofa, his hard leaking cock straining to get out of his now soaked jockstrap. Dan's need was too urgent for a gentle build up and Adam yelped as one, two and then three fingers hastily spread the lube into his hole without giving him proper time to adjust. He then felt empty as the fingers were withdrawn just as abruptly and he heard Dan fiddling with the buttons on his fly. Seconds later he was filled up again with Dan's beautiful, veined cock and felt the thick fabric of the jodhpurs rub against his still tender arse. Try as he might, Dan could not last more than a few minutes before erupting into Adam with a roar. After slumping over Adam for a while to regain his composure, Dan tenderly pulled out his still-hard cock and sat back in his armchair, wet dick hanging out of his button fly. Looking over his shoulder at his contented looking Master, Adam checked it was OK for him to move. Dan nodded and Adam slowly knelt before him again. Dan could see the soaked state of his jock and the red cockhead sticking out of the waistband. "You really need to cum, don't you slave boy?" said Dan, "Yes please Sir, please Master,"

was Adam's desperate reply. Dan bent down and
gently peeled off the sodden jock, then ordered Adam
to lie on his back on the floor, knees raised and feet
spread, soles flat on the floor. He then carefully slid
one boot under Adam's balls and rested the other on
his hairy chest. "Wank", was his final monosyllabic
order. The feeling of the leather under his balls was
too much and Adam shot almost immediately coating
himself and Dan's other boot with a shower of cum.
It was the most intense orgasm he had ever
experienced.

15 SARGE STU

Dan allowed Adam to rest on the floor for a few minutes before very gently nudging his balls with his boot. "Time to clean up, boy. Bring me a cloth to clean my dick when you're done". Adam struggled to his feet and wobbled towards the bathroom. Despite trying to clamp as hard as he could, he felt some of Dan's spunk running down the back of his legs and could not resist stopping in the bedroom en route to the bathroom to collect a small butt plug. Something made him want to keep Dan's seed inside himself for as long as possible, so he sealed it in with the plug before returning with a warm flannel to clean Dan's now softened cock. He lovingly wiped and dried it and was moving down to his master's boot to remove his own cooling cum from it with the used cloth, when Dan moved his foot away. "Not with the cloth", he whispered. Adam understood immediately, but hesitated as he considered how unpleasant the mix of cold jizz and boot polish would taste. Then he remembered the load of his master's still hot spunk trapped inside him with the butt plug and was once again determined to please him in whatever way he ordered. He knelt lower and licked the boot clean. The taste was not quite as bad as he imagined, but not one he would have chosen. The contented "good boy" from the deep voice above him did, however, make it all worthwhile.

Knowing that it was now less than 3 weeks until the end of lockdown and therefore until Kerry moved in and Dan resumed his straight life, Adam tried to savour every moment of living with and serving his Master full time. The ex-soldier did have some work to do each day, keeping in touch via Zoom or email with those of his security team who were still on assignment. Adam spent this time naked under Dan's desk, massaging his feet, or – if Dan was particularly bored on a long Zoom – gently suckling on his cock until he could log off and fuck his boy's face properly.

Given that Adam had previously run his own marketing company, he even surprised himself by how content it made him feel just to be naked at his Master's feet for hours on end. Most of the time he was entranced in a worshipping zone, comforted by the deep timbre of the confident voice above him, but sometimes he found himself tuning into Dan's meetings. After one particularly tense call, Dan wasted no time in taking his frustration out on Adam's throat and his slave thanked him for his load in the appropriate way by kissing the bare feet he had just been massaging for 40 minutes. "Sir," Adam ventured politely, "may I say something about that guy you were just speaking to in Florida?"

Dan looked down, puzzled. "Fire away", he replied. Adam explained that he didn't trust Richy, who was head of the small security team Dan supplied for a Florida billionaire on his Palm Beach estate. Richy had spent most of the call bitching about Dan's latest, British hire, who was now stranded in the US and apparently not pulling his weight. "It's funny, listening to the voice without seeing the face, gives you a different perspective and there was something about him that did not ring true," Adam concluded.

Dan nodded down at Adam, who was still on his knees, slightly flushed from the face-fucking. "Matt, who he is complaining about, is the younger brother of one of my best army mates and I definitely did not have him down as a slacker. I thought maybe lockdown thousands of miles from home had given him some mental health issues or something. I'm going to have a discreet word with the client. Thanks boy!"

The true situation became clear when Dan spoke to his usually pretty taciturn client a few hours later. He raved about Matt who had not only picked up on some gaps in the perimeter fence on his first day on the job, but had kept the billionaire's very bored teenage son from going stir crazy by coaching him in soccer on his days off. Dan understood that Richy's complaints were based on envy of the attention Matt was getting from the client's family and was able to smooth over the situation with a few quiet words to both employees.

After that, Adam spent less time under the desk and more time next to Dan, out of camera shot, but making notes and generally being helpful, but both roles pleased him inordinately. After all, there was plenty of time for him to be on his knees outside office hours…

Dan and Adam fell into a routine incorporating their Dom/sub roles with remarkable ease and they found a balance between 'normal' day-to-day living together and experimenting with kink scenarios that turned them both on enormously. Adam had thought that his man in riding boots and jodhpurs was about the hottest thing he had ever experienced until Dan came into the kitchen one evening in what he later described as his 'red carpet bodyguard outfit' – black Armani suit, crisp white shirt, black silk tie and an earpiece with a curly flex coming out of it. Adam, in his by now usual cooking attire of jockstrap and apron, almost came in his pouch at the site and remained achingly hard and drooling throughout the 'interrogation,' his wrists fastened to the back of a barstool by the black silk tie.

While Adam was living for the moment, trying to enjoy the experience with no expectation of ever having a permanent relationship with Dan, Dan was beginning to think more introspectively than he had ever had before. He was a man of action, a doer, but the situation he found himself in forced him to reassess everything about his life. His initial, violent reaction against the thought of being 'turned' gay by Adam had almost completely disappeared. It felt so right having sex with Adam and it felt even more right that he was in the completely dominant role. Adam made him hard, but also made the rest of his life - outside sex – more comfortable and relaxed than it had ever been. It couldn't be forever though, could it? What about Kelly? What about his daughter? What would his mates say?

He was pondering this one afternoon while Adam was working in the kitchen, when his mobile rang with "Stubs" as the caller ID - his old friend, Stu or Stubble or Stubs depending on the banter level. "All right Stubs, you old wanker?" was his cheery, if impolite greeting." Dan's smile faded as he heard his friend's reply, "not so good Danno. I know it's not allowed to be in each other's houses at the moment, but I need to talk. Can I come over a bit later?" Dan didn't hesitate. He and Stu had been through too much together in the army. "Course mate, come to the back gate of the building so the guys on reception don't see you. Bell me when you're there and I'll come and let you in."

Dan hung up and turned to Adam. Sorry babe, it's Stu – the mate from the army I told you about. He sounds in trouble, so he's coming over. I don't think it's the time to introduce him to my naked slave boy. You'd better go back to your place for a while. Adam nodded silently, disappointed to be leaving Dan even for a few hours, but secretly delighted at Dan's rare use of 'babe'. He put down his chopping knife and headed to the bedroom to put on more clothes.

Just as he came back into the living room, more modestly dressed in shorts and T-shirt, to say goodbye to Dan, a short, stocky figure made a surprisingly athletic leap over the glass balustrade of the balcony and strode into the flat through the open sliding door. Dan's "what the fuck?" was interrupted by a bear hug from the famous Stu. "Just keeping in practice for the ol' covert ops," he explained over Dan's shoulder.

Stu pulled back and turned to Adam, who saw Dan flinch a little at being cornered into an introduction he hadn't expected to make. "Stu, this is my neighbour Adam – he just came round to borrow a drill." Dan turned to Adam and added, "it's in the hall cupboard, mate. Help yourself on the way out." Adam took the hint and with an uncharacteristic "cheers, mate," turned to leave. Stu put his hand on Adam's shoulder. "Nah, stay for a drink – I need help with woman trouble and you'll probably be more use than this divorced fucker," he said, nodding his head in Dan's direction. Adam looked at Dan to see what he should do and with a slightly exasperated shrug of the shoulders, Dan agreed he should stay.

It was about an hour and several cans of strong lager down the road when the army joshing and anecdotes petered out and the real reason for Stu's visit emerged. Since leaving the army, he had suffered from PTSD, which had led to depression, gambling and the end of his first marriage. He pulled himself together, got a job as a nightclub bouncer and a new girlfriend, Amy. All was going well until she suggested moving in together. Stu had freaked out. He loved her, but worried he was still too 'fucked up in the head' for a live-in relationship.

Bolstered by the strong lager, Adam ventured some very wise advice about how Amy might be feeling and mis-understanding Stu's reluctance and that complete honesty with her about his own self-doubt would work wonders. Stu listened intently and said very seriously, "Adam, my new friend, you are a clever bloke and I am going to try that". His army façade soon kicked back in though, "got any whisky to celebrate, Danno?" he enquired cheekily of his old buddy.

One round of Scotch led to another and out of the blue, Stu suddenly changed tack again and said, "so tell me what's going on with you 2 and your (dramatic pause) *drilling?*"
Dan spluttered out a mouthful of whisky and Adam froze, like a rabbit in the headlights. 'We're together, sort of," said Dan calmly, much to Adam's astonishment. Equally calmly, Stu asked, "together in what way?" Adam edged forward on his seat, eager to know how Dan would describe their relationship. "Well, we're fucking and he's…," Dan paused at looked over at Adam, who made the tiniest of nods. "He's my slave".

Whenever Adam thought about it for years later, he was never sure if he or Dan was the more astonished at Stu's reply: "Fucking hot, can we piss on him?"

Dan was briefly lost for words. He didn't know whether he was more shocked by Stu's lack of concern that his friend was in a gay relationship, or his filthy suggestion. Once again, he looked over at Adam for his approval and this time the nod was more emphatic. Dan turned back to Stu and said, "rude not to share, right?" then to Adam, "naked on your knees in the shower NOW, boy!"

Adam, who had wanted to try water sports for years, but had never summoned up the courage to ask, was in position in less than a minute. He didn't have to wait long for the army buddies to march in, arms over each others' shoulders, fish their cocks out and let loose simultaneous, beery streams over his kneeling body and face.

As Stu finished and started to tuck his short, but impressively thick cock back into his pants, he shook his head in disbelief and muttered, "fucking hot" again. Turning to Dan he said, "time to go, I think my old mucker – see me out to the back gate. I've had too many whiskies to get over that fucking balcony and I've got to do the big chat with Amy in the morning."

Both friends left Adam to have a long, hot shower and he was just drying off as Dan came back in. He silently took the towel from Adam and led him by the hand to his bed. "Mmm, nice and clean now", he muttered as he started to kiss slowly down his boy's back, eventually coming down to his taut butt cheeks, parting them and embarking on his first ever rim job with gusto.

16 EPILOGUE

Adam was still in blissed-out state from the 3 way water sports session with 2 hot ex-soldiers, so the unexpected attention on his arse from Dan's firm tongue really was the icing on the cake and he could not hold back his moans of pleasure. Eventually he felt lubed fingers replace the tongue and he raised himself off the bed to show how much he wanted it. Dan slowly pulled his fingers out one at a time and Adam felt a very hard cock head pushing slowly, but determinedly into his hole. He realised very soon that Dan was making love to him for the first time, rather than just fucking him and he thought his heart would burst with joy. Although Adam's hard on was being ground into the mattress as Dan gradually picked up the pace, when Dan shot with a roar inside him, he didn't feel the need to cum himself, just revel in the thought of his master's seed inside him. Dan rolled off contentedly and they were both asleep in minutes.

Dan woke early the next morning and looked over at the handsome, younger man beside him. He knew immediately what he needed to do and stepped out onto the balcony to make a call without disturbing Adam. 40 minutes later he was walking around the communal garden of the building with Kelly, her greyhound in tow.

"Kelly, I'm going to come straight out with it," began Dan in a voice that sounded more confident than he felt. She put her hand up. "I know what you are going to say – you don't want me to move in with you." He nodded sadly, bracing himself for an outburst, which did not materialise. "I've known something wasn't right since before lockdown. I love you Dan, and I think you have a lot of affection for me, but it's not enough. The moving in plan was a kind of test….and now we have the result." He saw the pain in her eyes and turned to give her a hug, which she accepted, without hugging back. She pulled back, smiling weakly. "Anyway, we would have been hopeless long term – the strong, silent type is hot for a while, but I love a chat." Kelly turned towards the garden gate and, with a wave over her shoulder, said. "Good luck darlin'. I hope you find someone you really love." "You too babe," Dan called after her, thinking to himself, 'I already have'.

He launched up the steps to his flat 2 at a time and burst into the hall, shouting for Adam. Adam appeared at the bedroom door, red eyed. "Nearly finished packing," he announced in a shaky voice. "Why the fuck are you packing?" demanded Dan. "I saw you and Kelly all lovey dovey in the gardens. She wants to move in straight away, doesn't she? I'll be out in 15 minutes," Adam blurted out, trying desperately to hold back the tears and preserve a little dignity.

Dan immediately saw how the hug and quiet chat with his now ex-girlfriend could have been misinterpreted from a distance.

"We were breaking up…for good," he explained quietly. "So now I can be your full time, permanent Master…..and boyfriend."

It took a few before the unbelievably good news registered in Adam's brain and he flung himself into Dan's arms, saying 'I love you' over and over until Dan stopped him with a long kiss and said, "time to show me how grateful you are boy", pushing him gently to his knees.

The End